A Flock of Shoes

story by Sarah Tsiang ☺ art by Qin Leng

annick press
toronto + new york + vancouver

We acknowledge the support of the Canada Council for the Arts, the Ontario Arts Council, and the Government of Canada through the Book Publishing Industry Development Program (BPIDP) for our publishing activities.

ONTARIO ARTS COUNCIL
CONSEIL DES ARTS DE L'ONTARIO

Cataloging in Publication

Tsiang, Sarah
　　　A flock of shoes / by Sarah Tsiang ; illustrated by Qin Leng.

ISBN 978-1-55451-248-5 (pbk.).—ISBN 978-1-55451-249-2 (bound)

　　　I. Leng, Qin　II. Title.

PS8639.S583F56 2010　　　　jC813'.6　　　　C2010-900419-1

Distributed in Canada by:
Firefly Books Ltd.
66 Leek Crescent
Richmond Hill, ON
L4B 1H1

Published in the U.S.A. by Annick Press (U.S.) Ltd.
Distributed in the U.S.A. by:
Firefly Books (U.S.) Inc.
P.O. Box 1338
Ellicott Station
Buffalo, NY 14205

Printed in China.

Visit us at: www.annickpress.com
Visit Qin Leng at: www.qinleng.com

For my daughter, Abby, and for all the shoes that got away.
—S.T.

For my beloved parents and sister.
—Q.L.

Abby loved her sandals.

hi hi hi

Grrr...

They were pink and brown with lime green trim.

They were perfect for running

and walking

and skipping

and jumping.

When she hopped in them she felt light as air.

They made small heart tracks in the sand
and followed her all around the beach.
They invited the wind to come kiss her toes.

Abby and her sandals

had a wonderful summer together.

summer

But when fall came, her mother tried to take them away.

"Your feet will be too cold!"

"Your sandals are getting worn!"

"You're starting to outgrow those shoes!"

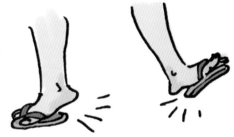

My mom is full of nonsense...

But Abby's mother was often full of nonsense.

One bright fall day at the park, Abby was swinging with her favorite sandals on. Abby was swinging higher than she had ever done before.

She swung so high that her
sandals flipped right off her feet,

first one,

then the other.

But her sandals didn't land with a plop on the sand.

And her sandals didn't land with a thunk on the grass.

Her sandals flipped and flopped in the sky, pretty as birds, and joined another couple of pairs of sandals, all in a V.

And when she told her mother,
her mother huffed about fibs and
got out Abby's brand new boots.

All winter long in her boots,
Abby thought about her sandals.

She wondered if they were making little hearts in white sand.

She thought about how the warm wind liked to tickle the open spots. She hoped they were getting enough exercise.

Wish you were here. The weather is warm, the sand is soft, but we still miss the tickle of your toes!

To Abby

Our straps are
aching to hug
you again.

To Abby

Eventually, around February, Abby began to really love her boots. They were white and blue and had a lovely trim of purple that went all around the edges.

They were great for stomping

and running

and kicking

and climbing.

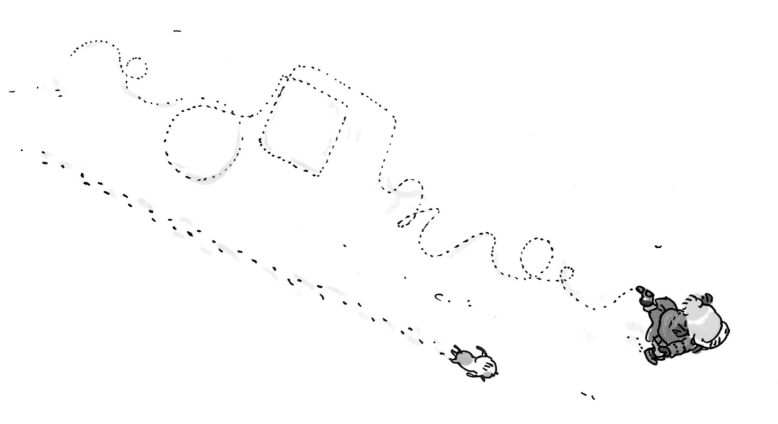

They made squiggles and squares
and tiny circle tracks in the snow.

They followed her all throughout the white woods.

They hugged her toes with their soft, fuzzy felt interior.

Then, one warm spring day as Abby
was putting on her sunscreen, she heard
the whistle of the north-bound train.

Her boots snapped to attention
and were out the door before
Abby could call to them.

She ran out after them in her bare feet,

but they were already joining a line of
rugged boots, running and hopping on
the boxcars as the train chugged by.

The sweet sound of harmonica music and the
beat of stomping boots floated on the breeze.

Abby sat in the new grass and waved sadly to her beloved boots.

Until she heard the
swish of flying sandals.

They landed gracefully from the sky, parting
from a large flock of shoes, and they were a
glorious pink and brown, with lime green trim.

They were rested and
fat, grown just wide
enough for _Abby_'s feet.